Clown, Bear
and
Rabbit

For my daughter Susan

First published in Great Britain in 2000
by Piccadilly Press Ltd, 5 Castle Road, London NW1 8PR

Text and illustrations copyright © Tony Maddox, 2000

A catalogue record for this book is available from the British Library

ISBN: 1 85340 578 7 hardback
1 85340 583 3 paperback

Printed and bound by Proost, Belgium

1 3 5 7 9 10 8 6 4 2

Text design by Louise Millar
Set in 20pt Celestia Antiqua

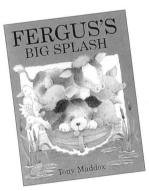
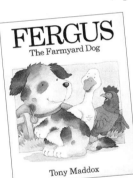
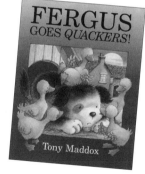
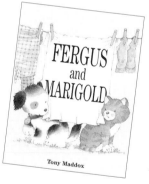
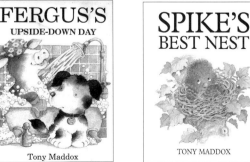

Tony Maddox lives in Worcestershire.
Piccadilly publish his wonderfully successful FERGUS series: FERGUS'S BIG SPLASH,
FERGUS THE FARMYARD DOG, FERGUS GOES QUACKERS!, FERGUS AND MARIGOLD
and FERGUS'S UPSIDE-DOWN DAY. They also publish his SPIKE book: SPIKE'S BEST NEST.

CLOWN, BEAR and RABBIT

TONY MADDOX

Piccadilly Press • London

Clown, Bear and Rabbit looked out from an upstairs window of the old house to the empty street below. They were looking for Granny.

"Where can she be?" said Bear.
"We haven't seen her for ages!"
"She must have forgotten about us," said Rabbit with a sigh.
"Perhaps she's downstairs," said Clown cheerfully.
"Let's go and see!"

The three friends wandered through the empty rooms. Everywhere was dusty and cobwebs hung from the ceiling. "It never used to be like this," whispered Bear. "And there's no sign of Granny," said Rabbit.

Suddenly they heard the front door open.
They peeped round the corner and saw
men carrying tins of paint and ladders
into the hallway.
"Quick!" whispered Clown. "I think
we had better hide!"
They scrambled into a large box and
covered themselves with newspapers.

It wasn't long before they felt the box
being lifted and carried away.
Then they were falling . . .

. . . on to something soft . . . and very smelly!
"Uuuurgh!" said Bear, wrinkling up his nose.
"Where are we?" asked Rabbit.
Clown looked around. "We're in a rubbish skip,"
he said. "Let's get out of here . . . fast!"

The three friends climbed down from the skip
and hid in the garden.
Bear was not very happy.

"What are we going to do now?" he grumbled.
"We haven't anywhere to live."
But Rabbit had just remembered something . . .
from a very long time ago.

"Follow me!" he said. He led them down the overgrown path to the bottom of the garden. "There!" he cried, pointing up into the big tree. "I knew it would still be here."

"It's the old tree-house!" said Bear excitedly. "We used to have picnics here with Granny's children!"

They climbed up the wooden ladder
and settled down in their new home.
Bear gave a big smile of relief.
"We'll be safe here," he said.

The weeks passed. Then one day the sky grew dark and they heard the rumble of thunder. Rain poured down and the tree-house began to rock in the strong wind. The three friends huddled together. They were joined by small birds and animals sheltering from the storm. "I wish we were back in Granny's house," said Bear. Clown and Rabbit agreed.

The next day they made their way back to the house.

"It's quiet. The men must have gone," said Rabbit.

He climbed up on Bear and Clown's shoulders to look through a small open window. "I can just squeeze in, and then I'll open the door for you."

Inside, the house gleamed like new. The three friends made their way up the stairs to the old nursery.

"Look!" cried Bear in surprise. "It's just like it used to be!"

"Even Rocky is back," said Rabbit happily, pointing to the wooden horse.

"I'm tired," yawned Clown. "Let's get some sleep. That storm kept me awake all night!"

They climbed into their old toy cupboard and fell sound asleep. They were woken by the sound of voices.

"Look what I've found, Mum!" said the small girl.

"Well, I never . . ." said Mum. "It's my old Bear! And Clown! And dear old Rabbit!

Granny must have kept them safe all these years."

"Can we look after them now?" asked the small boy.

"I'm sure they would like that," said Mum with a smile.

And Clown, Bear and Rabbit *did* like that very much indeed!